GRANDPA'S LITTLE ONE

For Lady J—watching you and the "little one" is magic
—B.C.

To Gabriela
—G.P.

Grandpa's Little One
Text copyright © 2006 by Billy Crystal
Illustrations copyright © 2006 by Billy Crystal and Byron Preiss Visual Publications, Inc.
Manufactured in China
All rights reserved.
No part of this book may be used or reproduced in any manner whatsoever without written permission
except in the case of brief quotations embodied in critical articles and reviews. For information address
HarperCollins Children's Books, a division of HarperCollins Publishers, 1350 Avenue of the Americas,
New York, NY 10019.
www.harperchildrens.com

Library of Congress Cataloging-in-Publication Data
Crystal, Billy.
   Grandpa's little one / Billy Crystal ; illustrated by Guy Porfirio.— 1st ed.
      p.   cm.
   Summary: A loving grandfather celebrates his grandchild's first birthday.
   ISBN-10: 0-06-078173-4 (trade bdg.) — ISBN-13: 978-0-06-078173-6 (trade bdg.)
   ISBN-10: 0-06-078174-2 (lib. bdg.) — ISBN-13: 978-0-06-078174-3 (lib. bdg.)
   [1. Grandfathers—Fiction. 2. Babies—Fiction. 3. Birthdays—Fiction. 4. Stories in rhyme.] I. Porfirio, Guy, ill. II. Title.
PZ8.3.C88647Hap 2006   2005014037
[E]—dc22   CIP
                                                                                                                                      AC

Typography by Jeanne L. Hogle
1 2 3 4 5 6 7 8 9 10
❖
First Edition

BILLY CRYSTAL

author of the bestselling I ALREADY KNOW I LOVE YOU

GRANDPA'S LITTLE ONE

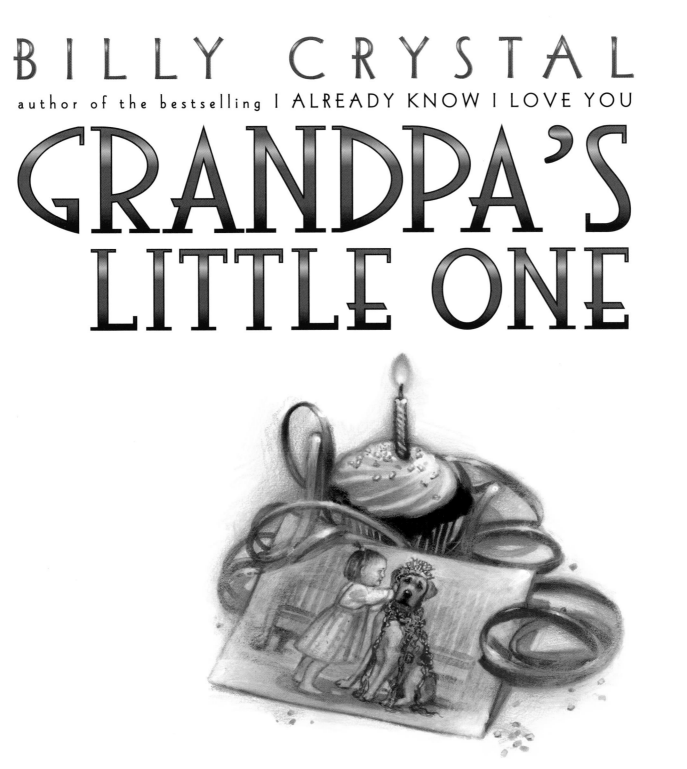

Illustrated by GUY PORFIRIO

HarperCollinsPublishers

Happy birthday, little sweet one,
you're one year old today.
I gave you your first piece of cake,
once Mommy said, "OK."

You didn't just eat it,
    you wiped it on your face.
Then you rubbed it on Daddy's nose—
    it went all over the place.

I'm glad it was hot out so we could
go swimming in the pool.
I love to watch you do new things—
all you used to do was drool.

You're learning all about your world,
and soon you'll start to walk.
You crawl, you laugh, you pull
yourself up,
and you try very hard to talk.

Right now you just make noises:
"goo goo" and "woo woo" too.
You cry whenever you're hungry,
and I cry when you poo.

You're eating grown-up food now;
   that baby stuff was yuck.
Grandma gave you pizza
   and ice cream from a truck.
To watch you eat your first ice cream,
   with it dripping on your chin,
was one of those special moments—
   all I could do was grin.

It all tastes so much better
than applesauce and rice.
I can't wait to give you
chocolate—
I know you'll think it's nice.

I wonder if you're thinking,
  Why does Grandpa talk that baby way?
I know I must look silly, but I do it anyway.
I have the feeling that you understand everything I say,
  like *granpa boo boo lee doo, la la la la la lay.*

You really like your toes a lot—
you found them yesterday.
Although you have a lot of toys,
it's with those toes you'd rather play.

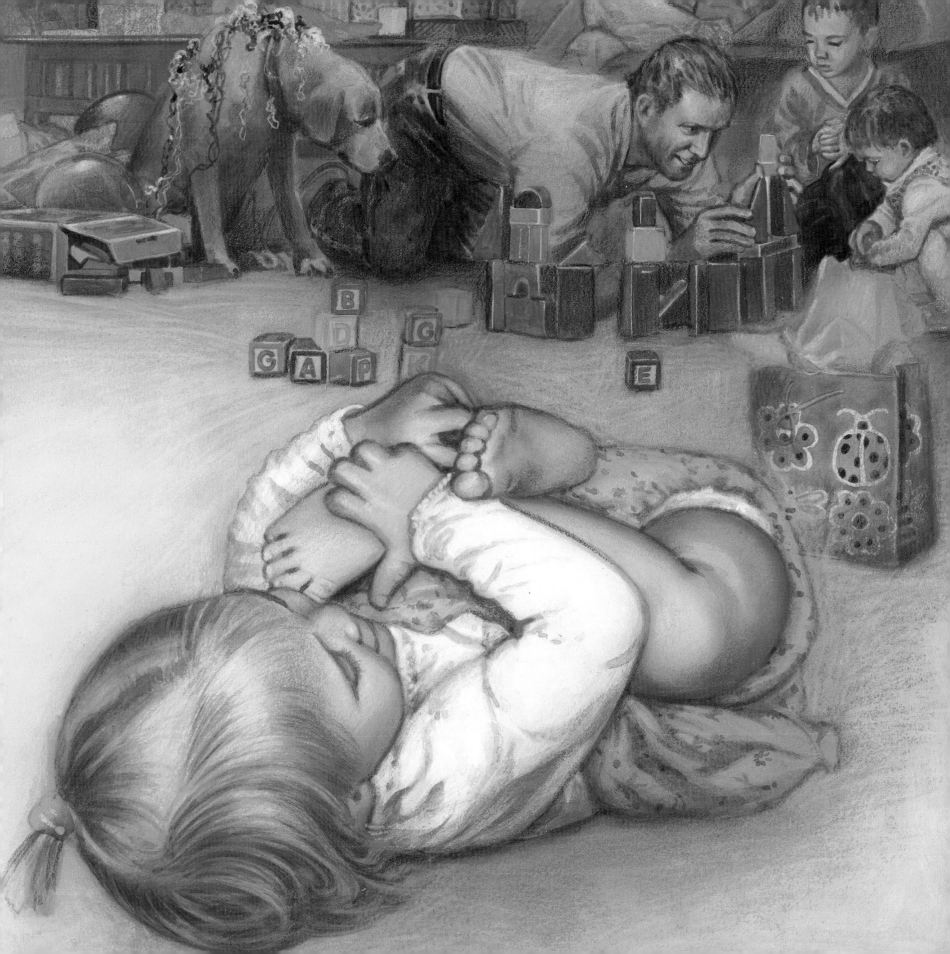

I watch your mommy hold you
and sing a lullaby.
I love it when you smile at her—
something's shiny in her eye.

I bring you to the mirror
and smile at what you do.
You giggle at the little girl
who looks the same as you.
You press your lips to the glass
and give yourself a kiss.
This year with you, my grandchild,
is time I'd never miss.

I've shown you where the clouds are,
   and you can point to the man in the moon.
We sing "Itsy Bitsy Spider,"
   and dance around the room.

This year has gone so quickly,
you've learned so very much.
One thing no one can ever teach
is the beauty of your touch.
When your little fingers rest upon my hand,
there's a feeling in my heart
only a grandpa can understand.

So good night, little sweet one,
what a perfect day for you.
One was fun—it surely was—
but I can't wait for two.